The Want Monsters

And How They Stopped Ruling My World

Chelo
Manchego

SHAMBHALA
Boulder 2016

Want Monsters come in all shapes,
sizes, and colors. Everybody has one.
All they want to do is make people happy,
but you'd better watch out because if
your Want Monster gets too big, you'll
be in big trouble!

This is Oskar, my **GINORMOUS** Want Monster.
It's not that he's bad; his wanting has given me
the strength to win races and the compassion to
help someone in need. But lately Oskar has gone
completely bonkers with some of my wants!

He has grown a big belly because when I eat a cupcake,
Oskar makes me want to eat four more . . .

And then I get sick.

He has lots of thumbs now
because when I play video games,
he makes me play until
my thumbs are sore . . .

And then even giving a high five hurts.

He has a crown on his head because when I get attention, he makes me want to be king **ALL the time.**

But even royalty needs to be alone from time to time. I am pretty popular already, and that extra "help" he gives me doesn't make me cooler at all. Sometimes it even does the opposite.

Don't get me wrong—I love Oskar—but it's
making me sad that it isn't easy for us to get along.
I think Oskar knows this because
he gave me a flower to cheer me up.

I discovered a little caterpillar hiding in the flower, and he asked me what was making me sad.

I said, "I have a Want Monster that makes me eat and play video games and want to be the center of attention way too much."

And then I asked him, "Do you have a big Want Monster too?"

The caterpillar looked at me with amusement. "Oh, no!" he said, "If caterpillars had big Want Monsters like humans do, we would eat all the trees in the world and never stop to turn into butterflies. That would be silly. But I want yummy leaves all the time and that's alright! You just have to know when to say *no más*!"

"I try to say *no más,* but Oskar, my **GINORMOUS** Want Monster, does not listen to me. I've tried fighting back, but he is too strong. I've tried running away, but he is too fast.

The little caterpillar was quiet. Eventually he said, "You should just let Oskar be Oskar then," and he disappeared into a bush to keep eating yummy leaves.

The next day I had an ice cream.

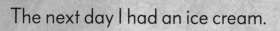

Oskar and his big belly
made me want to finish the
whole carton by myself.

It looked delicious, but
I remembered to let
Oskar be Oskar. I said,
"Oskar, if I eat this whole
carton of ice cream
by myself, I'll turn into a
snowman. Sometimes
the things we want are
not good for us."

Oskar had a tantrum, but I kept minding my day until
I forgot about this want. With time, so did Oskar.

The next day I bought the video game
"Zombies Ate My Teachers," the best, most
incredible video game in the entire universe!

A week and a half later, "Zombies Ate My Teachers: **TWO**" came out, and of course Oskar and his many thumbs dragged me to the games store.

Games

New zombies ate my teacher 2

The game looked fantastic, and Oskar wanted it **RIGHT AWAY,** but I said, "Oskar, I need a break from this game. If I don't, my eyes will simply pop off my face, and then I'll be the zombie. New games will always be coming out, so I doubt this one will make us happy for very long."

Oskar had a tantrum, but I kept minding my day until I forgot about this want. With time, so did Oskar.

Yesterday I saw on TV a girl who won a talent
contest by playing the tuba . . . with her nose!

Oskar and his crown got jealous
pretty quickly and made me
want to win a contest on TV too.

Even though it would be nice to have a crowd
chanting your name, especially when you
are as popular as I am, I said, "Oskar, we can't
have everything we want. Besides, playing
the tuba with your nose is just gross."

Oskar had a tantrum, but I kept
minding my day until I forgot about
this want. With time, so did Oskar.

Oskar is now a tiny Want Monster;
I call him *Oskarcito*, and he lives inside my
pocket. We are getting along much better.

We still have some want fights, but if I take a deep breath and I am patient with him, Oskarcito stops being so grumpy and demanding. I tell him that instead, he can try wanting things such as kindness and sharing, because when we give these a try, everyone feels good.

Every now and then Oskarcito
will make me do things his way,
and that's okay. I would never
want to be completely free of my
Want Monster. That would be
just another want!

I love my tiny Want Monster, and my
tiny Want Monster loves me back.

The End

Epilogue

Want Monsters come in all shapes and flavors,
dresses and places, tattles and battles.

What does your Want Monster look like,
and what does it usually want too much of?

Let's draw it and get to know it!

SHAMBHALA PUBLICATIONS, INC.
4720 Walnut Street
Boulder, CO 80301
www.shambhala.com

9 8 7 6 5 4 3 2 1

First Edition
Printed in China

∞ This edition is printed on acid-free paper that meets the
American National Standards Institute Z39.48 Standard.
♻ Shambhala makes every effort to print on recycled paper.
For more information please visit www.shambhala.com.

Distributed in the United States by Penguin Random House LLC
and in Canada by Random House of Canada Ltd

Designed by Liz Quan

LIBRARY OF CONGRESS CATALOGING-IN-PUBLICATION DATA
Names: Manchego, Chelo, author.

Title: The Want Monsters: and how they stopped ruling my world /
Chelo Manchego.

Description: First edition. | Boulder: Shambhala, 2016. | Summary:
A little boy learns to calm Oskar, his Want Monster, who urges him
to overeat, play video games too long, and be the center of attention.

Identifiers: LCCN 2015048461 |ISBN 9781611803655 (hardback)

Subjects: | CYAC: Emotions—Fiction. | Behavior—Fiction. | BISAC:
JUVENILLE FICTION / Social Issues / Emotions & Feelings. |
JUVENILLE FICTION / Social Issues / Values & Virtues. | JUVENILLE
FICTION / Monsters.

Classification: LCC PZ7.1.M3633 Wan 2016 | DDC [E]—dc23LC
record available at https://lccn.loc.gov/2015048461